EXTRATERRESTRIAL (ET) Search

My sincere thanks to the following people for their time, information, images and enthusiasm for this book:

Daniella Scalice, NASA Astrobiology Institute, USA

Robert Peters, NASA Terrestrial Planet Finder Project, USA

Brad McLain, Alien Earths Exhibition, USA

Denise Blazek, Adelaide, Australia

Dear Reader

What comes to your mind when someone mentions the possibility of extraterrestrial, or ET, life?

You may be reminded of the movie, *ET: The Extraterrestrial*. Or you may think of the many scientists who search the solar system for Earth-like planets where extraterrestrial life forms may exist.

> OUR UFO (UNIDENTIFIED FLYING OBJECT) ELIMINATION CHECKLIST IS ON PAGE 28.

In this book, you will meet three knowledgeable people involved in the search for extraterrestrial life: an astrobiology educator (on page 16), a planet hunter (on page 19) and an educator at the Alien Earths Exhibition (on page 25).

By the end of the book, ask yourself the question: "Are we really alone?"

Sharon Parsons

Contents

EXTRATERRESTRIAL (ET) Search

1 Extraterrestrial (ET) Science Fiction

We earthlings have long been fascinated by the possibility of extraterrestrial life inhabiting neighbouring planets, solar systems or galaxies. One way we have expressed this fascination is through science-fiction stories in books, comics, animation and film. Some of our most successful movies feature fictional extraterrestrial life forms. In many science-fiction movies, new technology creates special effects that draw us into amazing and highly imaginative ET worlds.

Hundreds of planets that could potentially support life have been discovered in our own galaxy.

Sun
Mercury
Venus
Earth
Mars
Jupiter
Saturn
Uranus
Neptune
Pluto (dwarf planet)

the solar system (distances and sizes are not to scale)

As this illustration from 1882 shows, space travel has fascinated humans for hundreds of years.

1977: The first *Star Wars* movie (originally released as *Star Wars* but renamed *Star Wars IV: A New Hope*) is the most successful in the series. *Star Wars* is a space opera set in a fictional galaxy from another time. It features space-age heroes, and robotic and humanoid alien characters that fight some amazing intergalactic battles as good pitches against evil.

SPACECRAFT LAUNCHED IN 1977, TOO!

Voyager 1 (September) and *Voyager 2* (August) were launched in 1977. See page 13 for more!

1982: *ET: The Extraterrestrial* is a science-fiction movie about a boy who meets an alien, ET, that is stranded on Earth. The boy and his siblings hide the friendly alien until they aid ET's return to his own planet.

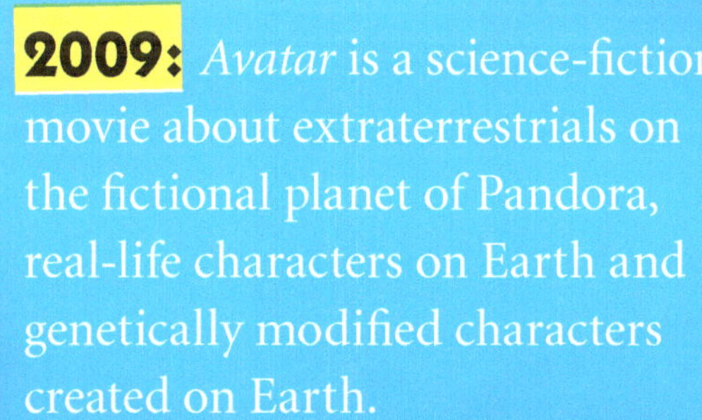

2009: *Avatar* is a science-fiction movie about extraterrestrials on the fictional planet of Pandora, real-life characters on Earth and genetically modified characters created on Earth.

Arts

Space Opera

Space opera is a highly imaginative fictional genre that includes science fiction. Stories are set in space and usually involve battles between powerful opponents.

2 Race to Space

Beyond science fiction, space science teams use their knowledge and technology to explore space and planetary systems for themselves.

Since the 1950s, Russia and the USA have had active space exploration programs that spend billions of dollars to employ people and to build spacecraft and space support resources, such as mission-control centres.

Yuri Gagarin undergoes training for his space flight.

Yuri Gagarin prepares for lift-off.

First Man in Space

The first person to travel into space, aboard *Vostok 1*, was Russian cosmonaut Yuri Gagarin in April 1961. After completing one orbit of Earth, Russian ground crew landed Gagarin's re-entry spacecraft by using remote controls. The flight lasted one hour and 48 minutes.

Valentina Tereshkova in her spacesuit

First Woman in Space

Two years later, in August 1963, Russian cosmonaut Valentina Tereshkova became the first woman to travel to space. Aboard *Vostok 6*, Tereshkova's flight lasted for almost three days. She was a parachutist before she trained as a cosmonaut.

COSMONAUT OR ASTRONAUT?

These job titles both relate to people trained to travel into space, but Russia refers to cosmonauts and the USA refers to astronauts.

I don't know why he is holding her ear!

Yuri Gagarin and Valentina Tereshkova

Social Studies

Space Jobs

There are many specialised jobs in space exploration organisations, such as astronauts, space scientists, engineers, technologists and technicians.

First US Citizen in Space

One month after Gagarin travelled into space (1961), astronaut Alan Shepard became the USA's first man to travel into space, on board the spacecraft *Freedom 7*.

In 1971, he was the spacecraft commander for his second flight into space, aboard *Apollo 14*.

About to Leave Earth

Alan Shepard prepares to travel into space.

the launch of Freedom 7

Oldest Man in Space

In 1962, John Glenn aboard spacecraft *Friendship 7* became the first US citizen and the third person in the world to orbit Earth.

In 1998, he also became the oldest astronaut to fly on a space shuttle – he was 77 years old.

About to Orbit Earth

John Glenn enters Friendship 7 *just before it is launched.*

Spacecraft velocity = about 28 000 kilometres an hour

Spacecraft mass = about 1 220 kilograms

the launch of Friendship 7

APOLLO 11

Apollo 11 was the first spacecraft to land on the Moon and its maximum velocity was almost 40 000 kilometres an hour.

The USA's First Woman in Space

In 1983, Sally Ride became the USA's first female astronaut to travel into space. She was aboard a space shuttle mission called orbital *Challenger* with four other astronauts. Today, Sally works on science education projects to inspire all students, especially girls, to explore the excitement of science, maths and physics.

First US Woman to Walk in Space

In 1984, Kathryn D. Sullivan walked in space. She completed three space missions in her career and was also a geologist.

Sally Ride on Challenger's *flight deck*

The space shuttle Challenger *orbits high above Earth.*

The USA's Youngest Astronaut

Sally Ride experiences weightlessness aboard Challenger. To date, she is the USA's youngest astronaut to travel into space, aged 32.

Social Studies

First Chinese Citizen in Space

In 2003, Yang Liewi made 14 orbits of Earth aboard Shenzhou 5. It was reported that he spoke to his wife from space and said, "I feel good, don't worry".

International Space Exploration

Since the early decades of Russian and American space exploration, other countries, such as China, Canada, France and the UK, have established space agencies, too.

3 Voyager Searches Space

The National Aeronautics and Space Agency (NASA) began operating in 1958. Since then it has been committed to finding out all kinds of things about our universe, including the question of extraterrestrial life. To do this, the agency has many research and space exploration projects, and also funds education projects about Earth and outer space in order to share its research and discoveries.

"The ultimate goal is to find Earth-like planets with atmosphere, evidence of biology and water."
NASA

This is Voyager 1. Voyager 1 *and* Voyager 2 *are identical spacecraft.*

Voyager 1 *begins its journey into deep space.*

Spacecraft Explore Space

In 1977, *Voyager 1* and *2* were launched into space by special rockets. These spacecraft were originally designed to explore space for about five years. But remote-control technology enabled NASA to upgrade its capabilities from Earth so that *Voyager 1* and *2* could continue their space research mission.

the gold-plated record that has travelled millions of kilometres into space

The *Voyager* spacecraft haven't "met" extraterrestrial life … yet!

A Gold Record

In case they ever do, NASA scientists have prepared for a possible meeting by packing a gold-plated copper phonograph disk on board each spacecraft. Each record is protected by an aluminium case and includes instructions in the form of easy-to-understand symbols that explain how to use the cartridge and needle to play the record.

The team collected a lot of information about Earth and recorded everything onto this gold record. It contains sounds and images of life on Earth, such as:

- natural sounds of animal life, weather and the environment
- musical sounds from many different cultures and time periods
- spoken and written messages in many languages.

4 In Search of Earth-Like Planets

What's an Earth-Like Planet?

NASA and other space agencies are in search of Earth-like planets. On Earth, all life forms use carbon molecules as their building blocks. Study the carbon diagram below to see how Earth's life forms are carbon based.

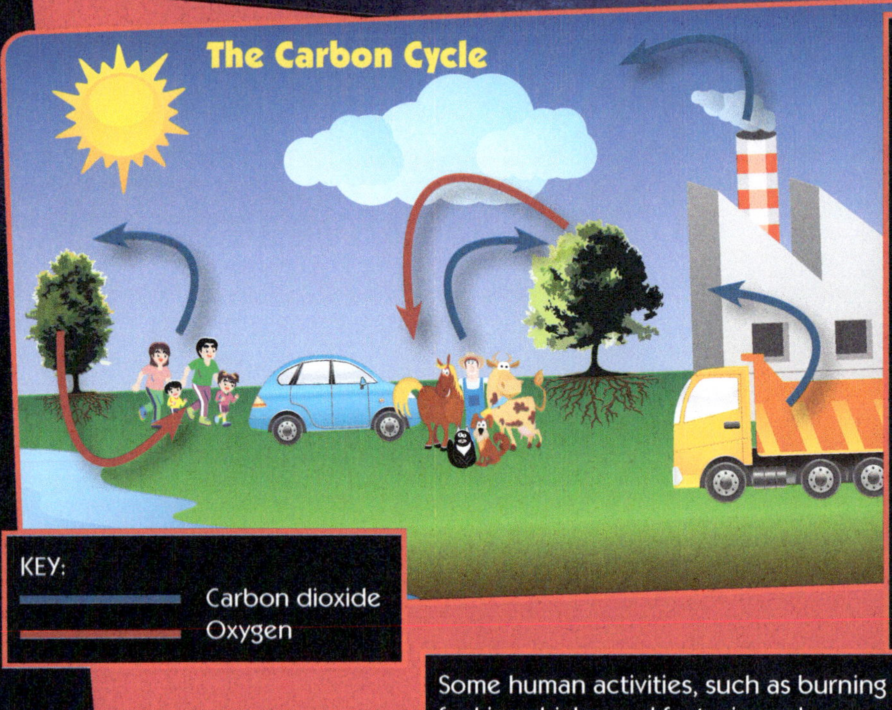

Humans and animals breathe in oxygen from the atmosphere. In their bodies, oxygen is used to "burn" food and release energy. As a result, oxygen and carbon are combined to form carbon dioxide, which they breathe out. Plants take in carbon dioxide. During photosynthesis, the plant uses the Sun's energy and the carbon in the carbon dioxide to create new sugars for energy. The oxygen is not needed and is released back into the atmosphere.

Some human activities, such as burning fuel in vehicles and factories, releases extra carbon dioxide into the atmosphere.

Most life on Earth also needs water, a range of temperatures in which it can survive, a mixture of gases it uses for its metabolism (oxygen for animals, carbon dioxide for plants) and an energy source to live and grow (plants use light, and plants are the basis for almost all food chains).

CARBON

After oxygen molecules, carbon molecules are the second most abundant in our bodies.

The Sun

The Sun is the key to creating the right conditions for living things based on carbon molecules to thrive. Earth is exactly the right distance from the Sun – not too hot, not too cold. The Sun provides light for plants to photosynthesise food.

Earth's Atmosphere

Over billions of years, during the formation of Earth, conditions were just right for an atmosphere to form and for water to form oceans.

Heat from the Sun takes about eight minutes to reach Earth.

Once the Sun's heat arrives, some is reflected off Earth and escapes into the atmosphere and beyond.

Some of the Sun's heat is reflected back to Earth by clouds and gases in the atmosphere.

What happens to the Sun's heat?

Astronomer Predictions

Within a thousand light-years from Earth, astronomers estimate there are at least 30 000 planets that are capable of sustaining life.

5 ET Search Via Astrobiology

In 1996, NASA set up an astrobiology department to research and collect data and images about planetary systems and possible life in the universe.

NASA began with three main questions.

1. How does life begin and evolve?
2. How does life exist elsewhere in the universe?
3. What is the future of life on Earth and beyond?

Daniella Educates in Astrobiology

Daniella Scalice works at the NASA Astrobiology Institute in the USA. Daniella helps people across the USA to learn more about the search for life elsewhere in the universe. She also works with scientists and educators to discuss ways of helping interested students become astrobiologists.

Science and Culture

Daniella has worked with the Navajo Nation – the largest Native American group in the USA – to create educational materials that help Navajo students learn that science and traditional culture can coexist.

Daniella (centre) and members of the Navajo Nation perform a dance depicting the formation of the solar system.

Daniella Enjoys Astrobiology

Daniella enjoys addressing the big questions of humanity: Where did we come from? Are we alone? These questions require scientists from many different disciplines, such as biology, astronomy and geology, to collaborate and respect one another's unique knowledge. Astrobiologists keep open minds in their search for life in our solar system and beyond.

NASA's Guide for Astrobiologists

NASA's seven science goals guide their astrobiologists in their quest to find out the answers to those three questions. Study the simplified list of their goals.

ASTROBIOLOGY

Astrobiology is a science that involves the study of the origin, development, distribution and future of life in our universe.

1. To understand the different kinds of habitable environments in our universe.
2. To explore our own solar system for habitable environments and life.
3. To understand how life forms began.
4. To find out how early life on Earth evolved with its changing environment.
5. To understand how life developed and evolved over time.
6. To think about what problems may affect life in the future.
7. To identify patterns of life in other worlds and on early Earth.

6 Exoplanet Missions

Exoplanets are planets that orbit stars outside our solar system. Space agencies around the world have discovered over 500 exoplanets, by using super-powered telescope technology and space missions. For example, the Hubble Space Telescope (since 1990) has been NASA's oldest and most successful science mission in helping us understand more about outer space activity.

EXOPLANETS OR EXTRASOLAR PLANETS?

Exoplanets are also known as extrasolar planets.

an artist's impression of the Phoenix *lander on the Martian surface*

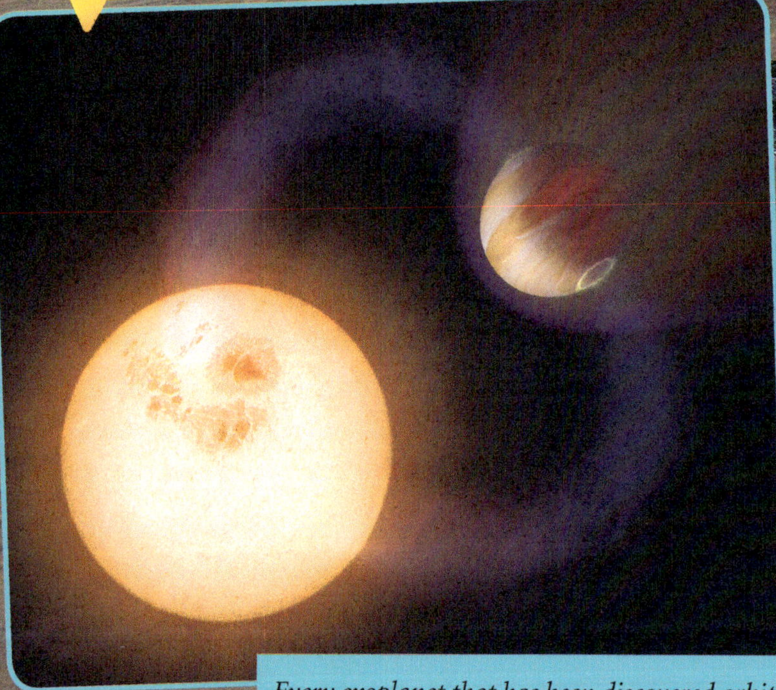

Every exoplanet that has been discovered orbits around a star or another gigantic planet.

Mars Missions

Mars is not an exoplanet as it is in Earth's solar system, but its exploration continues to be a key space mission for the future.

The *Phoenix* Mars lander, one of NASA's space landers, used its robotic arm to dig under the Martian surface. After digging about five centimetres below the surface, it found pure ice and rich soil capable of growing vegetables! This gives space scientists much hope of finding life forms on Mars.

IceBite

As part of NASA's preparation for future missions to Mars, the IceBite team works in the Antarctic because it has similar dry frozen soil (above the solid ice) to that of the north polar region of Mars. The team members work in the Antartic when they need to test new technology, such as robotic ice-penetrating drills in 2010.

The north polar region of Mars was chosen for landings because of a higher chance of finding water and evidence of life.

A Planet Hunter

Robert Peters is a NASA engineer who is also called a planet hunter because his work involves hunting for new planets. Robert works for the Terrestrial Planet Finder project, which involves a complex search for new worlds.

Robert Peters is a natural explorer. He enjoys many outdoor activities, such as geocaching and fly-fishing.

One complex technological system that Robert uses to find Earth-like planets is called an "adaptive nuller". In simple terms, it can block out light data coming in from a star and only collect data from its planets. This helps Robert to analyse a planet's atmosphere for elements that may sustain life, such as oxygen or water.

Recent **Space** Missions

2003: The Canadian Space Agency's first space telescope was launched inside a microsatellite from a cosmodrome in Russia. It is the smallest space telescope and it can study a single star for up to seven weeks at a time. This is useful because the telescope can watch for changes in the star's brightness, which can mean that an exoplanet is passing in front of the star. The telescope can make measurements that provide space scientists with clues about the size and mass of the exoplanet, and how far it orbits from the star.

The Kepler *mission searches for new planets.*

2006: The French space agency is called the *Centre National d'Études Spatiales*. It launched a space satellite to find large gas planets, small rocky Earth-like planets and more than 120 000 stars. Within six months of launching, the satellite discovered its first exoplanet.

2008: NASA "recycled" a satellite that was originally launched towards a comet in 2005. It is now used to search for new exoplanets, observe "wobbling" stars with planets and examine reflected light from other planets as part of the ultimate quest to find Earth-like planets.

2009: NASA launched *Kepler*, a discovery mission that searches our galaxy for Earth-like planets that have the conditions necessary to support life.

The Kepler *telescope begins its journey into space.*

Future **Space** Missions **(estimated dates)**

2012: The astrophysics division of NASA will launch a powerful space telescope to support the world's largest Earth-based telescope in Arizona, USA. Among its tasks, it will find planets, Earth-like planets and hopefully life beyond our solar system.

Scientists build the delicate mirror that will be used in the James Webb Space Telescope.

2012: The European Space Agency (ESA) will launch *Gaia*, a spacecraft designed to map our galaxy by using very high-powered telescopes. By the end of its mission it will have gathered information on about one billion stars, representing only one per cent of the Milky Way stars.

It is hoped that *Gaia* will also help NASA planet hunters locate Earth-like planets or worlds orbiting other stars.

an artist's impression of how the James Webb Space Telescope will look in space

2014: NASA expects to launch a very large space telescope to support or replace the Hubble Space Telescope. It is called the James Webb Space Telescope. Among its many jobs, the telescope will produce images of planets and planetary systems to determine their size and age. It will have a sun shield about the size of tennis court!

7 Zoom in on Young Planets

The W. M. Keck Observatory sits on top of Mauna Kea, a dormant volcano on the island of Hawaii. The scientific team there uses two powerful infrared optical telescopes to study fast-swirling dust and gas clouds called protoplanetary disks.

Scientists work inside the Keck Observatory.

the Keck Observatory

Studying Space

Their incredibly powerful telescopes enable the team to study the protoplanetary disks and stars that are about 15 million kilometres away. That's really close in astronomical terms!

One of the powerful telescopes peers through the skin of the observatory.

If the Sun was about the size of a bowling ball, Earth would be about the size of a grain of sand placed 25 metres away!

ASTRONOMICAL UNITS

One astronomical unit is about 150 million kilometres, which is the approximate distance between the Sun and Earth.

How Do New Planets Form?

The extreme energy generated by the swirling collections of disks can, over time, form or develop into new planetary systems. By knowing how new planetary systems form, scientists may get closer to finding out what "space ingredients" are required to form a habitable planet similar to Earth.

a view of the Hubble telescope from a space shuttle

From the Kuiper Belt, the Sun appears as a bright, but distant, star.

Hubble Finds Very Old Disks of Ice and Dust

In 2006, NASA's Hubble Space Telescope identified two very old disks of ice and dust – more than 300 million years old. They appeared to be similar to our solar system's Kuiper Belt. The disks are encircling stars that could have Earth-like planets. The disks are also old enough to have formed a fairly stable solar system that is similar to our much older solar system.

KUIPER BELT

The Kuiper Belt is our solar system's ring of ice outside the orbit of Neptune. Our solar system is about 4.6 billion years old.

8 Unusual Extremophile Discovered

In 2010, NASA's astrobiologists discovered a new bacteria that could survive in a lake containing arsenic, which is a toxic substance for all known living things. The astrobiologists discovered that this clever bacteria could survive on the harmful arsenic, instead of phosphorus (a helpful building block). All living things need many building blocks to live, including oxygen, water, hydrogen, carbon and sulphur.

Q: How is this discovery important for astrobiologists in search of extraterrestrial life on other planets?

A: This discovery means that life could thrive on toxic or poisonous elements on other planets – planets that are not like Earth.

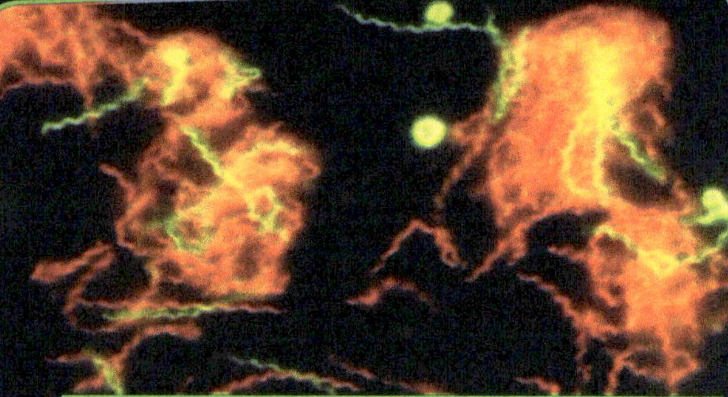

a microscopic image of an extremophile that lives in hot, acidic conditions

EXTREMOPHILES

Extremophiles are single-celled organisms called microbes that can live in extremely hot, dark or seemingly inhabitable places.

Earth Science

Think About This!

Just as life on Earth has adapted to the conditions here, life forms on other planets could have adapted to local conditions, too. Instead of being carbon-based like Earth's life forms, maybe they could be silica-based. Maybe they breathe ammonia instead of oxygen.

All living things on Earth have DNA – but maybe life forms on other planets use different molecules to create and sustain life.

This steaming hot crater lake in Yellowstone National Park, USA, is home to a wide range of extremophiles.

Alien **Earths** Education

Alien Earths is a US organisation that provides space education resources. Brad McLain is a biologist and a science educator who worked on the Alien Earths project. Brad enjoys educating people about the work that space scientists and astrobiolgists do in their search for extraterrestrial life in our solar system.

Children ask Brad many questions about whether aliens exist and what they might look like. He answers, "If aliens exist, they are unlikely to look like us, because they would have evolved on a different planet with different conditions".

Brad has worked with NASA astronauts, so he experienced zero-gravity training, too.

Brad made a video for NASA that involved "borrowing" R2-D2 to star as a virtual host character. R2-D2's role was to talk about astronaut life in space. The video was filmed at Skywalker Ranch – the workplace of Star Wars *creator, George Lucas.*

9 Listening for Alien Sounds

In the mountains of northern California is the Search for Extraterrestrial Intelligence (SETI) organisation. SETI has a team of about 150 scientists (including former NASA scientists) and their main task is to explore our galaxy for evidence of life. One way to do this is to search for signals from other planetary civilisations. So, in 2007, SETI began using its array of telescopes (made up of 42 massive antennas) to listen to or pick up any sounds in space that could be signals from intelligent extraterrestrial life. To date, SETI has not made any contact.

An array of radio telescopes scan the sky for signs of life.

an artist's impression of a remote astrobiology field laboratory looking for signs of life

Ancient Aliens

In 2010, the *History Channel* began screening a documentary series that investigated theories about Earth's contact experiences with human extraterrestrial life in ancient times. The program also featured people who believe that they have had one or more extraterrestrial encounters in today's world, too.

SCIENCE FEATURE

Are We Alone?

Earth is the only planet in the universe known to be able to support life. However, since earliest history, humans have looked into the night sky and wondered if we are alone.

UFO

What's That Unidentified Flying Object (UFO) in the Sky?

UFO Elimination Checklist

You see an unidentified object flying or flashing in the sky. What would you do? Try completing the UFO Elimination Checklist below.

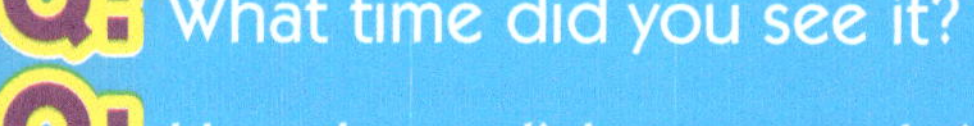

UFO QUESTIONS

Q: What time did you see it?

Q: How long did you watch it?

Q: What was its shape?

Q: What colour/s did you see?

Q: Was it moving or stationary?

Q: If it moved, was it fast or slow?

Could the UFO be …

- ☐ an aircraft
- ☐ a bird
- ☐ clouds
- ☐ fireworks
- ☐ a helicopter
- ☐ a hot air balloo
- ☐ a meteor
- ☐ a planet
- ☐ a satellite re-en aircraft
- ☐ a star
- ☐ a weather ballc

If you answered no to all of the items on the UFO Elimination Checklist, maybe you saw a UFO from another planet!

10 UFO Sightings Prove the Existence of Extraterrestrial Life

TEXT TYPE
Exposition
PAGES 29–31

"Welcome to another episode of *ETS*, the online program that invites Earth's expert-terrestrials to convince us that extraterrestrial life does exist in our solar system. The following report is from Debbie, who presents an argument for the existence of UFOs."

ETS

ETS (Extraterrestrial Search) is an acronym for a fictional online program on Earth.

astronauts Neil Armstrong, Michael Collins and Buzz Aldrin

Buzz Aldrin

Hundreds of people from around the world have used all forms of media to describe their experiences with extraterrestrial life or UFO spacecraft. However, reports from astronauts provide the most compelling evidence.

Aldrin's Account

Buzz Aldrin is one of the most famous astronauts to claim that he saw a UFO. He was the second man to walk on the Moon in 1969 as part of NASA's *Apollo 11* space flight. In an interview, Aldrin described a UFO encounter they had before *Apollo 11* landed on the Moon. Aldrin's fellow *Apollo 11* astronaut Michael Collins used a telescope to watch an L-shaped object flying alongside their spacecraft. But he was unable to make out what, exactly, the cylindrical object was. They wondered if it was the booster rocket that had left the spacecraft two days earlier. Commander Neil Armstrong asked Mission Control how far away the booster rocket was.

Mission Control Responds

Mission Control replied that the booster rocket was about 6 000 nautical miles (about 11 000 km) away from the spacecraft. But Aldrin did not think they were looking at anything that far away. After watching the L-shaped UFO for some time, the *Apollo 11* crew went to sleep and decided not to talk about it anymore.

These events told by the crew of *Apollo 11* prove that something is out there.

S–IVB

The S–IVB was *Apollo 11*'s *Saturn 4* booster rocket that left the spacecraft two days earlier.

APOLLO 11 UFO?

To date, the UFO reported by Aldrin has not been identified or confirmed.

History

Flag and Sign on the Moon

Neil Armstrong and Buzz Aldrin planted a US flag and a sign that read, "Here men from the planet Earth first set foot upon the Moon. July 1969 AD. We came in peace for all mankind."

the launch of Apollo 11

The US flag on the Moon was designed and built with wavy wire through it so it looked realistic.

Buzz Aldrin looks at the lunar lander.

Buzz Aldrin on the Moon

a historic first footprint upo the Moon's surface

Gordon Cooper's Account

A second report by another highly respected NASA astronaut, Gordon Cooper, backs up Aldrin's claim. While being interviewed on television, Cooper spoke about his personal encounters with UFOs. His first UFO encounter was in 1951 while he was flying for the US Air Force in Europe.

At that time, Cooper knew that the US military had the fastest and highest flying aircraft in the world. However, he reported seeing UFOs that were travelling at a much higher altitude. He described these UFOs as metallic, saucer-shaped craft that could do manoeuvres he had never seen before.

Gordon Cooper (1927–2004)

Gordon Cooper was a NASA astronaut who went to outer space aboard **Mercury 9** *in 1963 and* **Gemini 11** *in 1965. He was the first astronaut to orbit Earth 22 times, the first US astronaut to sleep in space and the last US astronaut to conduct a solo orbital mission.*

astronaut Gordon Cooper

Gordon Cooper Continues

Cooper made a later claim in 1958, when he was involved in a project that included tracking and filming aircraft in flight at a US military airbase. One day, while setting up their film equipment, Cooper's crew saw a saucer-shaped craft land nearby. They recorded the landing, using still and motion picture cameras. As they moved closer, the saucer lifted off and flew away at high speed. Once the crew developed the film, it was sent to headquarters as a top-secret file aboard a military plane. However, Cooper never received any follow-up and never found out what happened to the film.

Space Agencies' ET Search

Since then, many more NASA astronauts and pilots have shared their UFO experiences. Space agencies around the world invest billions of dollars in exploring space for all kinds of reasons. Perhaps the space agencies are also convinced that extraterrestrial life, in some form, does exist … out there in our universe!

Index

Glossary

cosmodrome A site for launching spacecraft

extraterrestrial Something that does not come from Earth and exists outside of Earth

metabolism All of the processes by which living things produce energy to survive

microsatellite An extra-small spacecraft that travels around a planet and records information to send back to Earth

protoplanetary disk Circle of gas and dust that surrounds a star and could form into a new planet

spacecraft Vehicles that can travel in space, including space shuttles, satellites and space probes

space telescope A device that uses lenses to make distant things look bigger and closer, and is launched on a spacecraft to observe objects in space

"wobbling" star A star that "wobbles" back and forth due to the gravitational pull of a planet orbiting it – the wobble helps scientists to discover new exoplanets